BUT THEN I REMEMBERED

by Chaya Leah Rothstein

pictures by Ruthy Perlstein

FELDHEIM PUBLISHERS

New York * Jerusalem

Dedicated to my parents—with love

In memory of Rabbi Sholom Goldstein, zt"l

for all that I remember . . .

First published 1990
ISBN 0-87306-963-8

Philipp Feldheim Inc. 200 Airport Executive Park, Spring Valley, NY 10977

Feldheim Publishers Ltd. POB 6525 / Jerusalem, Israel

Printed in Israel

It was a hot summer day. Most of my friends were outside with nothing to do. We were sitting in front of my house when we started to talk.

One of the kids said that he missed school.

Ovadia said he did, too, but there was a lot that he could learn at home. We all thought about that for a minute, and soon everyone had a story of his own to tell.

"One day a boy who was new in our school came up to me at lunch," said Ovadia. "He wanted to know if he could sit next to me. This new boy always looked messy. He always forgot his homework. He was never on time. No one usually paid much attention to him. I was about to say no to him, *but then I remembered . . .*

. . . a day when my father invited a guest to our house. The man looked funny. He kept forgetting where he'd put his glasses. And he'd come late for dinner. But my father didn't care. He treated our guest as if he were a King. I didn't really understand why.

MILK
MILK
MILK

"I looked back at the new boy. His eyes looked sad. I knew he didn't have many friends.

" 'Sit by me any time,' I said. Somehow lunch tasted better that day."

"I was in a rush to a baseball game one day," said Avrumi. "As I was about to cross the street, old Mr. Snow grabbed my arm. 'Avrumi,' he said, 'I'll cross with you, okay?'

"I looked at Mr. Snow in surprise. He walked so slowly, and I was in a hurry. I knew that if I didn't get to the game soon I wouldn't be picked for a team. I might not get to play at all. I started to say no, *but then I remembered . . .*

. . . my mother walking with my great-grandmother. She walked more slowly than Mr. Snow. But my mother always said, 'Take your time, Bubba Channa, take your time.' It always made Bubba Channa smile when she said that.

"I looked up at Mr. Snow. 'Take your time, Mr. Snow, take your time,' I said. Mr. Snow smiled and we crossed together."

"I was at the supermarket once," said Devorah, "and the lady at the cash register gave me too much change. I didn't count it until I was outside. It didn't seem to matter much by then. After all, the lady didn't know, so why should I bother giving back the extra money? I started to walk away, *but then I remembered . . .*

SUPER
M&G
MARKET
IN
IN
OUT

. . . my Zadie behind the counter in his butcher store. It was a busy day, and he had many customers at the same time. A lady had paid him too much for her purchases. My Zadie didn't realize it until she had already gone. Suddenly he raced out of the store and down the street. I couldn't believe it! I didn't know that such a small amount of money could be that important.

"I can still remember the lady's face when my Zadie caught up with her. She had been very impressed.

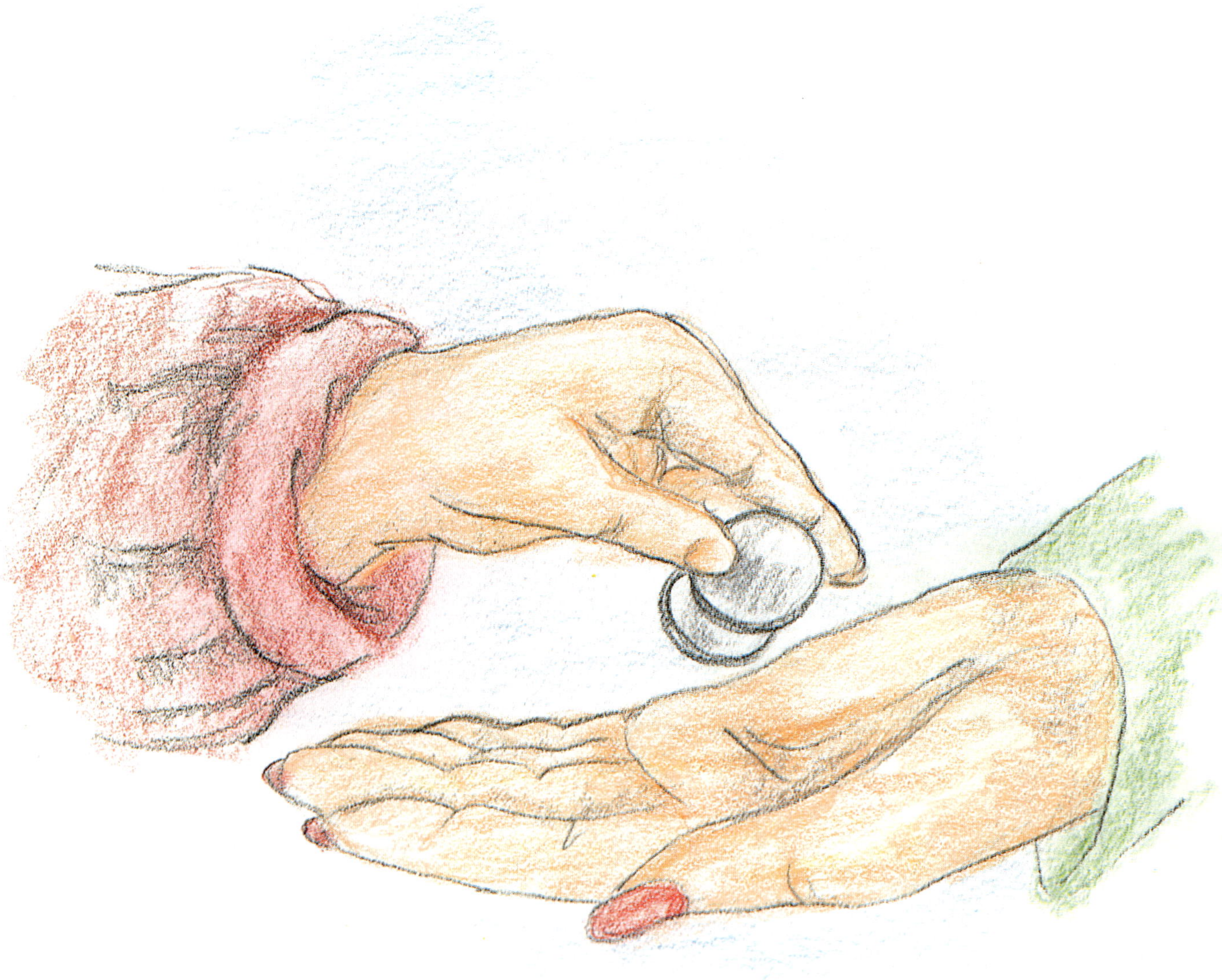

"Then, I knew what I had to do. I walked back into the supermarket and returned the change.

" 'This money is not mine,' I said."

"Sometimes I help my mother to prepare for Shabbos," said Shaindy. "On one Friday afternoon when it was very hot, my mother asked me to polish the candlesticks. It was a very difficult job. I started my cleaning, but I wasn't trying very hard. It wasn't easy to polish on such a hot day, *but then I remembered*. . .

. . . my Bubby kneading the Challah dough. She worked very hard when she did that. My Bubby's hands hurt almost all the time — but that didn't seem to matter when she made Challah. Her eyes would squint closed and she would softly sing, 'Lichvod Shabbos, Shabbos Kodesh.'

SILVER
POLISH

"I looked back at the candlesticks I was supposed to shine. It didn't seem to be as warm in the house as I had thought. Soon I was rubbing a little bit harder."

"Sometimes it's hard to know just the right thing to do," said Rafi. "Like the time my friend Shaya gave me a special candy. I wanted to eat it right away, but I wasn't sure which Brocho to make. It would've been so easy to simply pop it into my mouth. I almost did just that, *but then I remembered . . .*

. . . another time when I almost forgot to make a Brocho. I was near the milk machine at school. I had just bought ice-cold chocolate milk, and I was so thirsty that I almost drank without thinking. Suddenly I heard my principal's voice. 'It tastes even better with a Brocho,' he said, and he smiled. I had almost forgotten that time.

FRUIT STIX

"I looked down at the candy in my hand once more. It sure looked good, but I knew it would wait for a Brocho."

"There's a rule in my house about sharing," said Tuvya. "Everyone has to share what he has with everyone else. It does sound pretty fair, but it's not always so easy to do.

"One time my cousin Aaron came over. It was my turn to pass out the snacks, but there really wasn't enough for an extra person. I was just about to tell Aaron that we didn't have enough, *but then I remembered . . .*

. . . a Shabbos afternoon when I went to visit Sruli. His family was just about to have dessert. It was cherry pie, one of my favorites. I was hoping they would have enough for me. Then I realized that Sruli's mother was making all the pieces smaller. That way she could give me some too. I really felt good about that.

"I looked back at the snacks I was giving out and gave everyone a little bit less. 'There's plenty here for you, Aaron,' I said. And there was."

Suddenly there was quiet. Everyone had told a story. Everyone had shared a precious memory. We all sat there, thinking for awhile.

Then Ovadia said, "I wonder what my children will remember about me."

Glossary

Brocho: a blessing made before eating food
Bubba, Bubby: grandmother
Challah: special bread eaten at Sabbath meals
Lichvod Shabbos, Shabbos Kodesh: in honor of the holy Sabbath
Shabbos: Sabbath
Zadie: grandfather